Adam Mayer

Uncle
Tom

Aunt
Elsa

Edward
Wilson

John
Mayer

Frank

Mrs
Hale

Harriet
Hale

Agnes
Hale

Mr Hale

Dear Reader,

You have in your hands a packet of letters that have travelled **THOUSANDS** of miles. They have survived a **WORLD WAR**. They have survived journeys across the Atlantic Ocean filled with **ENEMY SUBMARINES**. They have survived **PESKY CENSORS** crossing out anything they think **SPIES** might find useful. They have **EVEN** survived **SNOOPING MOTHERS**. These letters are real survivors, just like Teddy — I mean Edward — and I.

Edward and I were best friends. We lived on the same street in Battersea, London in 1939 when Hitler and the Germans **INVADED** Poland, and Great Britain went to war. We played out together and even started our **VERY OWN COMIC BOOK**. Our favourite comic back then was the *Beano* and we wanted to make ours even better, with funny stories and brilliant artwork. Our comic book headquarters was in the Anderson shelter in my garden and we filled it with silly pictures of our friends and neighbours. But all that was before Edward was **EVACUATED** to the USA, leaving me to face the Blitz alone. Most of my other friends had been sent to the countryside, evacuated by the government to keep them out of harm's way in the city.

These letters show how Teddy and I fought our own battle to keep our friendship and our comic book alive, despite all the tragedy and change going on around us.

SPOILER ALERT: I never did get my *Beano* back!

Love,
Harriet

SILLY THINGS THE WAR IS MAKING PEOPLE DO.
BY HARRIET HALE (AGED 11)

Dig up their pretty gardens to grow **YUCKY TURNIPS.**

Break their ankles falling over while walking around in the pitch-black during a Blackout.

Say things like, **"JUST CARRY ON"**, when we could be invaded at any moment.

Send their children, including my **BEST FRIEND,** miles away for 'the duration' even though we have **NO IDEA** how long 'the duration' will be.

Paint their legs with **GRAVY** (I'm not joking).

Ration anything that tastes good. (You know they are never going to ration turnips.)

Stop chocolate factories from making chocolate and have them make **WEAPONS** instead.

Silly things about being evacuated to the USA.
By Edward Wilson (aged 11)

It is a **VERY** long way away.

People think **MY ACCENT** is funny
when I don't have one, they do.

They don't play cricket or
football (properly).

Maths They call maths 'math'.

They haven't joined the Brits fighting against Hitler.

They have **NO IDEA**
what pudding is.

They don't have the same comic
books. (Okay, theirs are pretty good too.)

I have yet to see a cowboy.

Dear Harriet,

By the time you read this, you will know that I have been evacuated. I am so sorry that I couldn't tell you about it. It was **VERY HARD** not to, but the people at the evacuation board made us promise. I wanted to tell you so badly that I swear I was about to **BURST**. You know I am a **TERRIBLE SECRET KEEPER**. Aren't you **AMAZED** I managed it? I suppose you're more angry than amazed.

I'm off to America for the rest of the war, or at least until things get safer. I didn't want to when Mother first suggested it. You know how we were glad not to be sent away with most of the other kids on our street during the first round of evacuations.[1] But then America just seemed like an adventure that was too good to pass up. This time next month I could be riding the range with

1 At the beginning of September 1939, it became clear that the United Kingdom would go to war with Germany. To keep them safe from the threat of bombings, over two million children were moved from their homes in cities and coastal towns across Great Britain to foster homes in the countryside, which were much less likely to be attacked.

real live cowboys! Mother said that was unlikely, but it is far more likely to happen if I go to America than if I stay here or get sent to a farm in Kent like most of the kids from our school. I will miss hanging out in your Anderson shelter[2] and writing our comic though.

I promise I will write to you with all of my news, whether I meet a cowboy or not. Will you write to me too and tell me about everything I will be missing out on at home? **PLEASE** say you will.

(Once you stop being angry of course.) You could be like my personal war correspondent!

2 People began building dugout shelters in their gardens, known as Anderson shelters, before war broke out in September 1939, but they didn't come into use in London for over a year.

Keep an eye on Mother for me, won't you? And Father
and Leonard when they come home on leave. Tell me
how they **REALLY** are. I know Mother won't want to
worry me. And do keep things going at comic book HQ!
We still need to think up a name! I'm promoting you to
EDITOR IN CHIEF. I'll keep drawing and writing.
Will you? I'll want to see everything when I get back.
Hopefully we will have enough for a few editions at
least. Perhaps I could add some American characters.

Your best friend, evacuee and future cowboy,
Teddy

P.S. If you weren't angry about me leaving without
telling you, I know you'll be angry about me taking your
new Beano! I am sorry, I just couldn't resist.

Dear Teddy,

YOU'VE GONE! I knocked for you this morning, but your mother told me you had run off to become a cowboy! Okay, that's not exactly what she said, through the sniffles. And then she gave me your letter. **AMERICA?!** I can't believe you **DIDN'T TELL ME**. I don't care what the evacuation board said, as my **BEST FRIEND**, who I played with **JUST YESTERDAY**, you **SHOULD HAVE TOLD ME**. And you definitely shouldn't have made off with my **NEW BEANO**.

What is it our warden, Mr Tavistock, always says? "Careless talk costs lives!"[3] Well I can tell you, no talk costs friendships (and by that, I mean not telling your very favourite people very important things that will affect **THEIR LIVES** as well as their comic collections).

Anyway, I guess you will probably be off the ship by the time you read this. I wonder how long this letter will take to get to you? I was ready to unleash a full Harriet Hailstorm when I read your note and only stopped stamping my feet and making a scene when your mother promised to forward my letters on to you with hers. She doesn't know exactly where in America you're going yet, but the evacuation board will send our letters on as soon as you're settled.

Your mother looked awful! She would hate me for telling you —

---

3 A phrase used on posters during World War Two, warning people to be careful what they say, as they could accidentally give away information to the enemy.

stiff upper lip, **"just carry on"** and all that. But how could she not be miserable? You are her little boy, even if I do think you are a **NO GOOD THIEF**. I felt you should know she was sad. Grown-ups are so strange at the moment, pretending that terrible things are **CHARACTER BUILDING** and that total disaster is something that brings out the best in people. It's as though they think Hitler will decide not to invade if we all keep pretending we are having a really good time.

She was as **MISERABLE** as when Leonard left for the RAF.[4] Do you remember? She didn't put her lipstick on for **TWO WHOLE DAYS**! I suppose I will have to just carry on without you. **UGH!** Make sure you write, or I will be even angrier when you get back.

Your *BEANO*-LESS best friend,
Hailstorm Harriet
Editor in Chief
P.S. You're right, we still need a name for our comic! How about **THE KEEP CALM AND CARRY ON?**

4 Royal Air Force

Edward Wilson

TO PARENTS OF CHILDREN REGISTERED FOR EVACUATION

DEAR SIR (MADAM),

Your child has now been registered for evacuation and the purpose of this letter is to notify you of the steps which it will be necessary for you to take before evacuation is ordered.

Clothes and equipment required by each child:

Gas mask
One overcoat or
mackintosh
One pullover or jersey
One shirt with collar
Two pairs of socks
One pair of trousers (long
or short)
One vest or combinations
One pair of pants

Handkerchiefs
One pair boots or shoes
One pair plimsolls
A comb
Toothbrush
Face-cloth
Towel
Stationery and pencil
Bible

Yours very truely,
L. G. ROSE
Evacuation Officer

Dear Harriet,

I've arrived in Liverpool. We are staying at a school until it is time to set sail, which should be soon. The journey hasn't been all that exciting, so far. A taxi came to pick me up very early in the morning and took me to the station. There I met with a teacher called Miss Rashbrook who travelled with us to Liverpool. There are fourteen of us in all, boys and girls. The youngest, Lionel, is five. The oldest (and doesn't she like to tell us) is Eloise who is fourteen. She reminds me of your sister, Agnes. She is a **REAL KNOW-IT-ALL**. You'd think she'd travelled all over the world, the way she talks. It turns out the furthest she's been is to the **ISLE OF WIGHT**!

We all had the same labels pinned to our overcoats with `American Committee for the Evacuation of Children' written on them, along with our names and other details such as who to contact if we wander off.

We carried suitcases and gas masks.[5] Though I don't think we will be needing gas masks when we get there. It will be funny not having to carry it around all the time.

We all sat together on the train. We had sandwiches and tea from the buffet car which was ace. More exciting than the soggy sarnies Mother always packs when we go anywhere anyway. The school has huge grounds which probably had nice lawns before they turned them into vegetable patches. They've left the cricket pitch alone though, so they have their priorities straight there.

5 Gas masks were given to everyone in Great Britain at the beginning of World War Two because the government believed that the German Airforce (called the Luftwaffe) might drop bombs containing poisoned gas on British towns and cities. People were advised to carry them everywhere they went, just in case.

The boys sleep in one dormitory and girls in another, which is across the corridor. **GOODBYE, ELOISE!** There were eight beds in our dorm, each with the same kind of scratchy grey blanket. The sheets were soft though. I've never slept in a room with so many people before. It felt rather strange. Everyone is in good spirits, although Lionel was a bit teary last night. I suppose bedtimes are hard when you are little. I told him stories about cowboys and read some of your *Beano* aloud, which seemed to calm him down.

Yours truly,
Teddy

P.S. Miss Rashbrook just told us that we will be sailing tomorrow! I will make sure to post this before we board.

Dear Teddy,

Sandwiches from the buffet car? This is already more exciting than any trip I have ever been on. Mother always packs lunch when we go to visit Agnes. I'm glad Eloise is along for the journey or you would be having far too much fun. Eloise is the kind of travel companion you deserve after not telling me you were going. **ONLY TEASING**! I'm not as angry any more.

How long does it take to get to America? It really is a **VERY LONG** way isn't it? I suppose it can't be helped. I thought I would dash you off a quick letter to tell you something **VERY FUNNY** that I worried I might forget about before I saw you next. Which would be a real **WARTIME TRAGEDY!**

You will never guess who the latest casualty of the Blackout has been.[6] Only our Warden,[7] Mr Tavistock, himself! He broke his **BACKSIDE!** His actual **BOTTOM BONE** – or tailbone as he likes to say. Now he has to sit on a special pillow like a **RUBBER RING** and everything. He was patrolling the street when he didn't see a car coming until it was **TOO LATE**. He managed to leap out of its way, but he cracked his

6 The Blackout meant that at night, doors and windows had to be covered, and streetlights and car headlights turned off. This was to stop the German Air Force from being able to use lights from the ground to see where to go. But living in the dark caused an increase in accidents across Britain!

7 Wardens made sure that people were prepared for air raids and reported any bombing incidents. They manned the sirens, made sure people had gas masks, knew where to go in the event of an air raid and patrolled to make sure that nobody was 'showing a light'.

BOTTOM on the curb. The fuss he made! He was louder than an air-raid siren. The Germans would have been able to hear him from across the Channel. Perhaps he scared them off... He won't be out of action though. Unfortunately, it only hurts to sit down, so he is now busy-bodying on doctor's orders. **UGH!**

Anyway, I thought it would make a great addition to *The Keep Calm and Carry On.*

Write to me when you get there! I want to hear all about it.

Harriet

Dear Harriet,

Hope you are well! I'm in New York, or the **BIG
APPLE!** I've no idea why they call it that. It looks
nothing like an apple. We survived the voyage from
Liverpool pretty well. Some of the group got seasick,
but I didn't. I was glad because the ship was lots of
fun for those of us that weren't hugging the heads.[8] We
played on deck most days and even saw an **ICEBERG!**
I didn't think it looked very big, but one of the crew
told me that it was probably **FORTY FEET HIGH!**
Not only that, but nearly nine-tenths of an iceberg is
below the surface. Did you know that? I didn't.

New York looks like a wonderland. Lit up with signs
advertising theatre shows, restaurants and all kinds of
BRILLIANT things to buy. I don't think I ever saw
London looking that bright, even before the Blackout.

8 The toilet on a ship is called the head.

I'm so used to everything being pitch-black outside that it made me nervous at first. Mr Tavistock's head would **EXPLODE** if he saw it. You know the way that vein bulges out of his forehead if he spots so much as a crack of light escaping.

PUT THAT LIGHTOUT!

Well, New York was lit up as if to say, "Come and get us! And while you are here, why not stop and enjoy and nice Coca Cola, buy a new vacuum cleaner or even see a show?" But it was us evacuees that were the real show! We caused quite the stir. **FAMOUS PEOPLE** were there to welcome us, or at least people I was told were very famous, some were real live **MOVIE**

STARS apparently, though I didn't recognize them from any movies I'd seen down at the Pavilion Picture Palace. The photographers from the newspapers couldn't get enough. **FLASH BULBS** popping wherever I looked made the city even more dazzling. Newspaper reporters asked some of us questions, like "How'd ya like the Big Apple?" I said something silly about looking forward to meeting a real cowboy. New York might not look like an apple, but I went as **RED** as one! Urgh. I hope they don't print it. Poor mother, sending me all

EVACUEES ARRIVE SAFE AND SOUND!

Edward Wilson (aged 12) said "I can't wait to meet a real cowboy!" Edward was in New York before taking the train to Dayton, Ohio. Where he is unlikely to meet a cowboy, but is likely to receive a very warm welcome.

the way over here to be safe, only for me to die of embarrassment in my first week.

We spent two nights in a boarding house and a few of us are due to take a train to Ohio tomorrow. I'm going to a place called Dayton. I hope you got my letter from Liverpool. Perhaps I'll even have a reply waiting for me when I get to Ohio! I need to get this in the mail! (They call post mail here.)

I promise to write when I get there. I've no idea how long this letter will take to get to you!

Your famous friend,

Teddy

Dear Teddy,

I just got your letter from New York! It sounds so exciting. I thought you were ignoring me, but it seems everything just takes an **AWFULLY** long time to travel across the pond.[9] You probably won't have got any of my letters yet, but I was SO relieved to hear from you after the news we've just heard. As soon as I read in the paper about a ship carrying evacuees, the SS *City of Benares,* being torpedoed by a German U-boat,[10] I thought I would be sick. I ran straight to your house. Your mother looked as white as a sheet, but she said she had checked and your ship had arrived safely. We gave each other a big, long hug. Oh, Teddy I was so frightened.

Things aren't very good here, either. They have started bombing London. I'm not sure if you get news from Great Britain over there. It's so far away and I am sure they have a lot of news of their own. I will do my best to keep you informed. There have been some very newsworthy goings-on in Battersea. The air-raid sirens sound almost every night and so we have to sleep in the shelter.

9 In real life, letters across the Atlantic would have taken a lot longer than this to arrive at their destination. Letters could take up to eight weeks and some, such as those carried on ships like the SS *City of Benares*, never made it.

10 On 17th September 1940 the SS *City of Benares*, a ship carrying British evacuees across the Atlantic, was torpedoed by a German submarine. Of the ninety children on board only thirteen survived.

The first night it was hard to get any sleep at all. I was listening out for every little noise. I clung as closely to Mother as possible (don't call me sappy, IT'S REALLY SCARY). I know Father is doing an important job fighting in Africa, but I would feel safer if he were here with us. It's the same every night. The rumble of the aircraft overhead grows steadily louder and louder until it sounds as if they are right over us. And then there are the bombs. When they land far away they make a kind of **CRUMP** sound. But when they are close, like they were the other night, it's more of a **BOOM** and the whole shelter shakes. Then there's the **ACK-ACK-ACK** of the anti-aircraft guns and the **DONG, DONG, DONG** of the bells on the fire engines going out to stop the fires before they spread. It feels like it's never going to end. I fall asleep eventually and am woken up by the **WAIL** of the all-clear siren. It's all very, very **LOUD.**

Stepping out of the shelter is scary, too. You don't know what you are going to find. Our street hasn't been hit, but streets nearby have. Do you remember Kenneth Whittle from our class? He's still safe in the countryside, but I saw his parents looking through the rubble of their home after a raid. I was helping Mother with the WVS canteen serving tea and sandwiches.[11] The Whittles said they were looking to see if they could pick out any keepsakes. It was horrible. Their lovely home looked like a stage set from the theatre. Half the building has come down, but the pictures were still on the walls, the blankets were on the beds and pans were in the scullery sink, waiting to be washed. Mother said it was yet another reason to keep the house looking spick

---

11 The Women's Voluntary Service helped provided food and other help for those who had lost their homes in the air raids.

and span, you never know when the whole street will get to see that you've not done the washing-up. Grown-ups are so **ODD**!

Even Buckingham Palace has been bombed![12] There were pictures in the paper of the queen standing outside her very own bombed house. So it seems no one is safe! I think it is very decent of the royal family to stay in London. They've so many fancy houses in the countryside, they could go **ANYWHERE** and be away from the bombing. Mother thinks they're sending a strong message to the Germans that we're all in this together and we are **NOT** afraid.

Goodness, I can't believe I almost forgot to write the most exciting

---

12 During the Blitz, Buckingham Palace and its grounds were bombed sixteen times, nine of which were direct hits.

part! I saw the **PRIME MINISTER**! Winston Churchill! I bet he's even more famous than the **MOVIE STARS** you met in New York, **HA!** He came to Battersea to see the damage done by the bombing. He walked through the rubble and broken glass with a crowd around him. He really does look like a **GRUMPY BULLDOG.** I thought he would look shocked at the many houses that had been blown to smithereens, but if he was he didn't give any sign of it. He didn't stay long, I suppose he had very important work to get back to, but everyone was very excited to see him and the fact he was so calm and determined made me feel like I should act the same.

The most thrilling thing to happen in the silly war so far and you missed it! I guess it serves you right for sneaking off with my comic in the night.

This is going to annoy you too — I've had to clear out our comic-book HQ because we are using the shelter most nights now. Don't worry, I've found the perfect spot for all our drafts and drawings — in Agnes' wardrobe! She took most of her things with her when she went to help Aunt Lucy with her **'VERY IMPORTANT'** war work in Buckinghamshire. (I'm rolling my eyes, can you tell?) She said she didn't know how long her 'services' would be needed. (Even bigger eye roll.) I am sure Aunt Lucy is doing frightfully important things (she's an absolute whiz at maths!) but what <u>**VERY IMPORTANT**</u> war work could **AGNES POSSIBLY** be doing?

EEEK, that's the siren going again so that's enough from me. It's strange, after the first couple of nights struggling to sleep down there, I'm now so tired I can sleep like a log. Even with Mother's snoring!

From,
Harriet

P.S. Your mother said you were living with a family called 'Mayer'? That sounds like a German name... Are you sure they're not **SPIES?** I asked your mother and she got all grumpy and told me not to be so silly. But are you **SURE?**

Dear Harriet,

Well, I'm here, and I haven't had any letters from you yet. I wonder if you've got any of mine. It was a **LOOONG** train ride. I didn't think it would be looking on a map. I didn't realize how big America is! The train went pretty fast but it took more than twice as long to get to Dayton than it did to go and see mother's cousins up in Aberdeen! I'm staying with Mr and Mrs Mayer, though they insist I call them Aunt Elsa and Uncle Tom. It feels strange calling them aunt and uncle when they aren't related to me, but we agreed Mr and Mrs sounded too formal, and Tom and Elsa sounded a bit impolite. They are very nice and say they hope that we will become like family, which is kind, but everything still feels a bit odd.

I'm sharing a room with Adam, who is fourteen. They have an older son, John, who has just finished university (which they call college). John is planning to join the navy in November so he said I could have his room then, but I don't think I'll need it as I'm sure the bombings will have stopped and I'll be on my way home by then.

And guess what? They DO have comic books here. Adam is very friendly and says I am welcome to look at his collection whenever I like! His favourite series is Action Comics which has this brilliant character called **SUPERMAN** in it! Superman is very strong with lots of **REALLY BIG MUSCLES** and can **LIFT CARS** and **FLY** and everything. I think we should have someone like Superman in our comic. Perhaps he could be called **CAPTAIN CRICKET BAT!** A boy who can knock twenty German planes out of the sky with a single thwack of his Britainium cricket ball. (Britainium is a super-strong metal I just made up.) What do you think?

I am due to start school next week. I've not unpacked properly though as I don't think I will be here that long. As soon as it's time to come home, I want to be ready to go. I really don't think it will more than a few months, do you?

Aunt Elsa just called me down for dinner! Promise I'll write more soon. I hope you'll write back!

From,
Edward

P.S. I am calling myself Edward here. I'm smaller than all the other boys my age and I think it makes me sound more grown up.

P.P.S. The Mayers have a lovely big house with a bathroom inside! They don't mind how high I fill the bath or how long I shower for! No more five-inch tubs for me.[13]

---

13 In 1939 most people in Britain didn't have bathrooms inside their homes. They had toilets in their yards and would wash in a metal tub, usually in front of the fire. During World War Two, the British government advised people to draw lines around the inside of their tubs to ensure baths were no more than five inches deep.

30th September, 1940
Dayton, Ohio

Dear Harriet,

Me again! I got your letters AT LAST! Not a word for weeks and then, just like buses, a whole pile land at once. First of all, I think "The Keep Calm and Carry On" is a **BRILLIANT** title. I'm annoyed I didn't think of it myself. Perhaps Captain Cricket Bat could be nicknamed **CAPTAIN CALM** whose superpower is to remain calm and stop for tea breaks no matter how crazy things get around him. Nothing frightens him, nothing makes him angry, he is ... **CAPTAIN CALM**. He sounds like the opposite of Hailstorm Harriet, doesn't he?

And **NO** Harriet, I do **NOT** think the Mayers are spies. Their ancestors were German, and they do like some German things like Bratwurst (sausages) and schnitzel, but there are lots of German Americans in Ohio. In fact, a couple of hours down the road, Uncle Tom said there is a place that changed its name to

North Canton from New Berlin after the last war. But that **DOES NOT** make them German spies, Harriet!

We did get the horrible news about the sinking of the Benares. Aunt Elsa doesn't think they will be sending any more children over either. She said it was a real shame seeing how **CHARMING** I was, and how many families she knew wanted to help an evacuee from Great Britain. Everyone seems to think I'm charming here! **ICK!** Uncle Tom and I were in the drugstore (what they call the chemist) and the man behind the counter said how much he liked my accent. I turned pillar-box red, began stuttering about how I didn't like how I spoke at all. It was all **VERY** awkward. Afterwards, over dinner, Uncle Tom told Aunt Elsa about it and they laughed. They said that when someone says something nice about you, all you have to say is, "**THANK YOU**". That sounds terribly **BIG-HEADED** to me. Can you imagine that at home? If your mother told my mother she liked her dress and your mother just said, "Thank you." Hah! Not very British, is it?

What this old thing? Why I found it at the dump under a pile of rotten turnips.

There are other differences too – like the funny way they use their knives and forks. They cut all their food up first and then PUT DOWN their knife and eat with their fork. Weird! I get lots of food here. In fact, I think I am putting on weight already as my short trousers are starting to feel tight around the middle. I can eat as much as I want of whatever I want and it feels wonderful. Yummy white bread and butter, meat, sausages, potatoes. **YUM!** I wish we could have you over for tea. And they have different sweets too. My favourites are Tootsie Rolls which are a bit like a soft toffee. I will be sure to bring some back for you when I come home.

I'm settling in well. The family have a dachshund called Frank which is short for Frankfurter. He doesn't seem to like me that much though. I wonder if it is because he has a German name? I am making it my mission to make him like me. And before you ask – **NO!** **I DO NOT** think **FRANK** is a **SPY**. Though I think it would be pretty neat if he was! A double agent dachshund.

I've started school in the seventh grade. I am much smaller and much skinnier than the other kids my age,[14] but they have all been very nice to me for the most part. Though they don't stop talking about my accent! And can you believe it, **THEY DON'T THINK THEY HAVE ACCENTS?** They say that they talk **NORMALLY** and that I sound like the **KING OF ENGLAND.** In fact, the whole 'Edward' thing has gone a bit wrong. Some of the boys have taken to calling me 'King Edward' which makes me feel a bit like a potato. I told Adam this and he laughed and called me 'Little Spud', which was even worse, so I guess I will stick with King Edward for now.

The school is much bigger than ours, even before the evacuations, and the subjects are different; but the work isn't too hard. I sit next to boy called Otto who has been friendly. He doesn't call me King Edward and hasn't done an impression of my accent once. He is really helpful when I need things explaining to me and doesn't roll his eyes like I'm being a dunce. One thing that needed explaining was the pledge of allegiance. They do it every day at the start of school.

---

14 Edward would be thinner and shorter than most kids his age in America because of his wartime diet. Lots of evacuees reported putting on weight when they arrived in the USA.

Everyone stands up and raises their right hand to the flag and says,

"I pledge allegiance to the Flag of the United States of America and to the Republic for which it stands, one nation, indivisible, with liberty and justice for all." [15]

Do you want to know something TERRIBLE about my new school? It DOES NOT have a cricket team which, apart from being away from home, is probably the VERY WORST thing about living here.

I'm sorry to hear about the bombings. The air raids sound really terrifying – it's no wonder you're afraid! I'm sorry I'm not there to hide in the Anderson shelter with you, we could have worked on the comic. We hear about what's happening in Britain on the wireless.[16] The reporter, Edward Murrow, is very good. Not least because we have the same name! At the end of each broadcast he says, "Goodnight and good luck." I guess it must feel like that when you go to bed, not knowing

---

15 The 'flag' or the 'Bellamy salute' began in 1892 but fell out of favour when Italian and German fascists used a similar salute for their leaders. It was officially replaced by putting a hand over the heart in 1942.

16 In 1940, people got their news from the radio, known as a wireless, or from newspapers. No smart phones or televisions for Edward and Harriet.

what's going to happen in the night. I am going to sign off my letters like that. Please do what you can to stay safe and please keep an eye on Mother.

Good night and good luck,

Edward

Dear Teddy,

Or should I call you, Your Royal Highness? Or perhaps Little Spud? Your letter made me laugh so hard I **ALMOST** spat out my tea. Luckily, I managed not to as it had the last of the sugar ration in it, and I would not have heard the end of it. Sorry about the name thing, I hope it blows over soon. I can't believe people think you are charming over there. You must have changed **A LOT** already. Only joking, I'm just jealous. I'll admit, my mouth was watering when I read about all the food you were getting. I like the sound of the Tootsie Rolls the best! It's still all-you-can-eat turnips,[17] mystery meat and national loaf here. I don't know why they call it national loaf. Putting the word national or victory in front of something does not make it taste better.[18]

Things are pretty bad here and it's not just the food. I'm **NEVER** going into the shelter again. It might sound crazy, but after you hear what happened in the Underground on Monday night, you will know I'm safer above ground. I've told Mother and I just don't care what she says. I went full Hailstorm Harriet when she tried to make me go in the shelter this evening.

The sirens went off at about eight o'clock. Mother and I were

17 Unfortunately, turnips were easy to grow and were not rationed. People really could eat as many as they liked.

18 'National loaf' or 'victory loaf' was a bread made of wholemeal flour with added vitamins, introduced because of white flour shortages. It was grey, mushy and quite yucky.

on the bus on our way home from running a canteen with the WVS. We weren't sure where to shelter, so we got off the bus, ran to Balham Underground Station and joined a crowd of people filing down the stairs onto the platforms. The underground felt so much safer than our silly tin shelter in the garden, and it was less damp, too. Mother gave me some tea from her flask and we shared a leftover sandwich.

The **CRUMPS** of the bombs falling felt further away, because we were deep underground. I was tired after the long day helping mother with the WVS, so I tried to get some sleep. Then I woke up to a **NIGHTMARE**. There was the **LOUDEST** bang I've **EVER** heard. A bomb had struck the tunnel and burst the water main. The tunnel was filling with water and people began to PANIC. I definitely didn't feel safe any more. We were trapped! There were so many people blocking the way out, **PUSHING** and **SHOVING** and **PANICKING**. We needed to **GET OUT** before the water rose and we all drowned, but we couldn't. I was **ABSOLUTELY TERRIFIED**.

I clung to Mother's hand as were swept along by the tide of people behind us, pushing us up the stairs over lots of poor people that had fallen down. There were so many of us struggling to get out that I was sure the air would be crushed out of my lungs. My hand's shaking as I write this, can you tell? The next thing I remember is waking up on the pavement and staring at the back of a bus that had toppled into an enormous hole in the ground. The Underground station had caved in! One thing is for sure, Teddy, I am not going underground again, not in a tube station and not even in our Anderson shelter. Let Hitler drop as many bombs on my head as he likes, I would prefer to be blown to smithereens than trampled to death. The newspaper said more than sixty people died in the water or in the crush to get out. They've not

BALHAM STATION A BOMBSITE!

said much about it though, it's hard for people to keep calm if they hear horrible news like that.

Yours,
Harriet

23rd October 1940
Dayton, Ohio

Dear Harriet,

Oh Harriet, I can't imagine how scared you must have been, I'm so glad you made it out. You must have been terrified. I wish I'd been there. I know it sounds crazy, but I do. If I had been there we could have escaped together. I could have pretended to be Captain Calm and squeezed your hand and told you everything was going to be okay. Or we could have put it all in a funny comic book strip and ended up laughing the way we always did. Nothing seems as bad when you find a way to laugh at it.

You are being so brave living with all of this going on. I'm not surprised you don't want to crush into the shelter, but I wish you would. I can't help but think that this is what Hitler wants. To make everyone so scared that they don't keep themselves safe and he can just march in and take everything.

When I listen to the news on the wireless, it makes me feel awful, knowing what you are all going through at home. We listen to Edward Murrow and I can hear the familiar noise of London in the background, the sirens, the bombs. Aunt Elsa says she feels like she is there and Uncle Tom thinks that if anything is going to make Americans join the war, these broadcasts are. I don't feel like I am there at all. I feel like I am **VERY FAR AWAY** and like I'm not a part of anything. You can play your part though Harriet, by being there and by staying safe too. Do say you will try to go down to the shelter.

Something to cheer you up, and maybe even rival your meeting with Mr Churchill... I saw **THE**

PRESIDENT! President Franklin Delano Roosevelt himself came to visit Dayton, Ohio. There I was, thinking that I was **MISSING OUT** on all the history-making by being sent out of harm's way, when a carload, or should I say a motorcade, of history comes streaking right by me. We had gone to the shops and were just wondering why the streets were so full of people, when there he was!

He was driven through downtown, waving from an open-topped car. I waved and waved and you will never guess who was sitting next to him, the first ever flying ace, Orville Wright himself. **ORVILLE WRIGHT!** One of the brothers that invented the aeroplane. The Wright brothers were from Dayton. Did you know that? I was so excited, you know how aeroplane-mad I am. Or `airplane' as they say over here!

Here's a photograph from the local newspaper!

Can you imagine being the first person ever to fly? He must feel like some kind of superhero! I definitely want to be a flying ace like Leonard and Orville now. I wish I could fly. I'd fly over to London and pick you up for a **ROUND-THE-WORLD TRIP!** I've written to Leonard about it – I thought he'd like to know that I'd seen the first man to ever fly one of the contraptions he cuts up the sky with. I hope Mother will pass on the letter to him when he is next on leave.

I can't believe I saw the president and the first ever real-life superhero flying ace! I can't wait to tell everyone at school, though I am not sure they will believe me.

Goodnight and good luck,

Edward

29th October 1940
Battersea

Dear Teddy,

You saw the **PRESIDENT! WOW**. I don't suppose you got the chance to ask him whether he was planning to give us any help over here at some point? Though if you had asked him, I can't imagine the shade of red you would have gone. They would probably have to invent a whole new colour to describe it. Only kidding. That is AMAZING.

The siren went again last night. It does every night at the moment. I pretended I couldn't hear it, but Mother came to get me out of bed and down to the shelter. I said I wasn't going and she couldn't make me. Thank goodness I'm too big for her to carry now. We sheltered under the dining table, the one we inherited from my great grandmother. It's made from solid oak so I think we were as safe there as anywhere. If the table has survived this long, it's going to survive Hitler. Mother didn't look convinced, but I wasn't stopping her from going out to the shelter.

We huddled together under there and were quite cosy. I think she secretly liked not having to go out and try and get warm under damp blankets. She said this was the last time though. We shall see!

Agnes thought we were crazy and went out to the shelter with

45

her blanket. She is home for a few days and is as **UNBEARABLE** as ever. Apparently, Aunt Lucy is working even more now, coming home at all hours. Agnes is there to help her around the house and keep up with her studies away from London, but you think it was her doing the **"IMPORTANT WORK"** with Aunt Lucy, rather than fixing meals and digging up potatoes.

She did bring something rather fun home though! Chicks! Four **FLUFFY YELLOW CHICKS** from the farm she has been helping out at. She said lots of people keep chickens to help make their rations go further. You lose your egg ration but you get an extra grain ration for the hens. I said I thought it was a most **EGG-SHELLENT** opportunity. [19]

Mother was less than pleased. She says she doesn't know where we will keep them, what with the lawn having been made into a ginormous vegetable patch. [20] I said we should keep them in the **'SHELL'-TER**. I'm not going to **'PLUCK'** up the courage to go down there any time soon. I think it would make a cracking **'HEN QUARTERS'**. She ignored that. Anyway, she said she'd ask Mr Tavistock if he knew of anyone who might be able to build us a little coop for them in return for some eggs. Let's hope he can **SCRAMBLE** something together. Get it? Scramble?

The chicks are so fluffy and cute. I've gone quite soppy over them. They are not the kitten I've wanted for forever, but they are the closest I'll get for now.

19 Many people took up this egg-shellent opportunity including the Savoy Hotel in London, which ran its own chicken farm inside the hotel to make sure its guests always had enough eggs for their full English breakfasts.

20 The government started a campaign called 'Dig for Victory' which encouraged everybody to keep their own allotment and grow as much of their own food as possible.

DIG FOR VICTORY

I'm the cluckiest girl ever!

I'm sorry you feel far away. I feel like you are far away too, except when I read your letters or when I am writing to you. Then it feels like you are right here.

From,
Harriet

Dear Harriet,

I can just picture your mother's face with the chickens! Hah! You will be quite the farmer by the time I get back. Your **YOLKS** crack me up!

It's been an egg-citing time here. Franklin Roosevelt won the election and gets to stay president! Uncle Tom and Aunt Elsa went to a big election party tonight. I think they are really pleased. I am too. I feel especially loyal to him after seeing him and knowing he is such a friend to Great Britain.

And we've had Halloween! Halloween is a **BIG DEAL** here! Everyone dresses up, it's brilliant. People spend ages working on their costumes. I swear Adam has been talking about his since I arrived. I went as Orville Wright, which was Adam's idea because I've not stopped talking about him since we saw him drive past. It was **A LOT** of work, but I really wanted to make myself an aeroplane. Not a real one, I wish! I made it from cardboard, it goes over my head and hangs over my shoulders with braces. For flying goggles, I cut up my gas mask. I was pretty pleased with it! Uncle Tom helped me make a propeller on the front that can really spin.

Adam was a swamp monster with green tentacles and Otto was Superman with lots of pretend muscles under his suit. Otto has become quite a good pal. He lives just down the street and likes lots of things I like, though he isn't very good at drawing. He does like comics though and thinks your drawings are ace! We all thought we looked pretty great in our costumes. We even made a mini Superman costume for Frank! Aunt Elsa took our picture and said we were sure to scare the neighbours senseless, which I thought was silly as my costume wasn't scary at all! I suppose she was being funny. I'll send you a picture when she has had them developed.

Here is a sketch for now.

After we got dressed we went from house to house saying "trick or treat" and helped ourselves to big bowls filled with candy, though some people gave us apples which wasn't as fun. We had a good time until we got to one house where a man dressed as an Egyptian mummy said he thought my costume was **THE BEST** he'd seen. I wish I hadn't cut the rest of my gas mask off. It would have hidden how red I went! I must have looked like some kind of flying beetroot! I managed to mumble, "Thank you." I'm not sure I'll ever get used to that.

When I get home, we will go trick or treating, though I'm not sure our mothers and fathers will like it much. They'd call it begging, which it kind of is, but it is very good fun.

I hope you're going into the shelter during the raids by now, Harriet. Your grandmother's table isn't strong enough to stop Hitler! You'd be weird if you weren't scared. But you have a duty to your country to be scared silly in as **SAFE A PLACE AS POSSIBLE**, and that is the 'shell'-ter. The Hailstorm Harriet I know was no chicken, even if she has started to keep them. Please say you will think about it.

Good night and good cluck,
Edward

P.S. It's a good job they make a big deal about Halloween here. Can you believe it, they don't have Bonfire Night?

Dear Teddy,

I saw your brother Leonard! He was home for just a couple of nights. Your mother was beside herself as it was a big surprise. He looked thinner and about five years older, if that's possible. I only saw him a couple of months ago. I suppose they have been working him very hard.

I was so excited to see him so I could tell you all his news — and he did have some wonderful news! He said the 'Battle of Britain' is over. Don't get too excited — we're still at war and being bombed and everything, but it looks like Hitler won't be invading England any time soon.

Hitler was trying to destroy the Royal Air Force so that he could invade. Hah! My pals and I showed them it's not how many planes you have, it's what you do with them. We outflew them and won. Hitler won't be marching down Oxford Street any time soon.

You should be very proud of your brother, Edward. I know I am. A real hero. I'm sure your mother was proud of him too, but she was too busy trying to feed him and make him rest and telling him off for making her worry. You'd have thought he was a helpless baby bird instead of a heroic flying ace.

But you didn't finish your dinner!

I thought you might like a bit of good news. Hah! I suppose I don't send you very much of that.

Agnes was home too from ███████████████████████████
███
███
████████████ 21

21 Whatever was written here has been deleted by the censors. Letters across the Atlantic were often read by people known as censors who would use a thick blue pencil to cross out any information that could be used by the enemy, such as locations of searchlights, nature of war work and dates of important raids, you know, just in case the Mayers were spies.

She said she had brought some important papers home with her. Stuff Aunt Lucy had asked her to practise so that she might be able to help out one day. She kept patting her suitcase as though she had **REAL MILITARY SECRETS** in there. I took a look while she was hanging up the laundry. All that was in there was lots of crosswords puzzles. Very important indeed... She is so annoying! Big, enormous eye roll.

AND ANOTHER THING, know-it-all Agnes really does NOT know it all. Do you remember the four fluffy chicks that she brought from Aunt Lucy's? Well we won't be getting many eggs from them as three out of the four are growing into very fine **COCKERELS!** Let's hope she is better at helping Aunt Lucy with her **VERY IMPORTANT** war work because she is positively featherbrained when it comes to farming.

Mother was finally starting to like them, but then they started doing what cockerels do — **CROWING.** Mrs Edmunds said the noise was worse than the sirens. She had just got baby Constance to sleep after the last all-clear when they started their morning **COCK-A-DOODLE TO-DOING**. You should have seen how quickly she was in our yard. She said if we don't cock-a-doodle do something about it soon she would **WRING THEIR NECKS** herself. I thought that was a bit unfair and was about to go full **HAILSTORM HARRIET** at her when mother grabbed my shoulders. She told me afterwards that Mrs Edmunds had had a telegram that Mr Edmunds plane had come down and that they weren't sure where he was. I am very sad for Mrs Edmunds, but I don't think our cockerels are to blame.

Mother now says they have to go, but she said we could get more chickens to keep Henrietta company (that's what I named the hen!). What do you think I should call the others?

I have a new friend besides Henrietta. Do you remember the Adlers? They moved in just before you left I think. They escaped here from Poland after Hitler invaded. I didn't like them at first because I thought they had strange accents that sounded German. I would pull faces at their daughter, Irena, whenever she walked by and wouldn't let her play in the street games. Well I wouldn't until Mother found out. **GOODNESS**, she was angry! She said the Adlers were Polish and had more right to **HATE HITLER** than anyone else on our street. She said Hitler was doing some horrible things to people in Poland, especially Jewish people like the Adlers.[22] She said the Adlers had made a **VERY DANGEROUS** journey all the way across Europe and that the last thing Irena needed was a girl like me being horrible.

Imagine **COMING HERE** because it is safer. With all the bombs?

I play with Irena sometimes now. Her English is really good, but I am helping her with the names for things they didn't have in Poland like jam roly-poly and hopscotch. She is pretty good at drawing too. She might be able to join our comic book. Irena doesn't talk about the journey much, but said they left in the night and she had to leave most of her toys. The only thing she took was her doll, Agata. Agata looks a bit of a mess if you ask me, but Irena treats her like she is made of glass and won't let me

22 The Nazis had lots of horrible beliefs. They thought that certain groups of people were less than human, including Jewish people. They rounded these people up and sent them to terrible prisons called concentration camps. Millions of people died in these camps.

touch her. She said her grandmother gave it to her. Her grandparents were too old to make the journey and are still in Poland. I think she worries about them a lot.

From,
Harriet

P.S. I know they seem like very nice people, but you have lived with them for a bit longer now. Are you sure the Mayers are not spies? With all the talk of Agnes's very important work, I just thought I would check again.

Dear Harriet,

The Mayers **ARE DEFINITELY NOT NAZI SPIES.** I don't like the Nazis any more than you do, but I don't think they are **STUPID.** What would be the point in putting all of your spies in Ohio? We are nowhere near Washington, or anywhere else involved in the war and it's not like I can give them any information. And how's this for you? Uncle Tom used to be a doctor in the US Navy in the last war. That should tell you whose side they are on.

I can't believe you got to see Leonard. I am **VERY** proud of him. I hope now the Battle of Britain is over he won't have to work so hard. Mother wrote that she thought he looked very tired.

What could Agnes be wanting with all those puzzles? I would say she was a woman of mystery but she would **LOVE** that!

We just had Thanksgiving and it was **BRILLIANT**. A lot like Christmas without all the presents. It's a big holiday where people celebrate the Pilgrims' first harvest in America.[23] We had a big dinner with an **ENORMOUS TURKEY** and **BUTTERY MASHED POTATO**. I ate so much you'd think I wouldn't have room for pudding, but Aunt Elsa said that she had made an **EXTRA SPECIAL SURPRISE** for me, so I knew I'd find room somewhere.

I always thought we spoke the same language, but I now say for sure we **DO NOT**, and I know this because of Aunt Elsa's extra special surprise. It's sort of my fault. Aunt Elsa asked me last week what my favourite food was in England. I said I couldn't remember the last time I had a good steak and kidney pudding, and that it was my absolute **FAVOURITE**. It turns out that Americans have no idea that pudding isn't always a dessert.

Well, I will give Aunt Elsa top marks for effort. She came out with her tray of little glass dishes. Each filled

23 White settlers from Europe.

to the brim with something brown and topped with what looked like **WHIPPED CREAM.**

I made your favourite dessert - steak and kidney pudding. I put a little cream on top!

I didn't know what to say so I thought, what would Churchill do, picked up my spoon and took a big bite. It was **DISGUSTING!** Gritty and grainy with lumpy bits of kidney. I didn't know what to do! **I DID NOT** want another mouthful but I didn't want to be rude. I thought I was going to have to eat the whole thing! But then Uncle Tom tried a bit and spat it all back out.

"Is it supposed to taste like this?" he asked, coughing.

"Erm, it's usually meat with gravy, wrapped in pastry," I said. "It's not usually sweet. And definitely no cream. Well, in fact, it's not really a dessert in England, but this is ... erm, quite tasty too..."

Uncle Tom started laughing and then Aunt Elsa began to laugh. She took a small bite and then spat it into her napkin.

"Edward, why didn't you say something?" she said. "I do believe you would have eaten the whole thing. You must speak up when something is wrong. Dear boy, your manners will be the death of you. What on earth are we going to do with all this disgusting pudding?"

That's when I remembered Frank. I took my dish to the kitchen and emptied it into Frank's bowl. Frank sniffed at it and ate it all in two big gulps. I think I will be Mr Popular with him from now on. Never mind Thanksgiving, you'd think all of Frank's Christmases had come at once!

Uncle Tom said, seeing how thankful Frank was for his `pudding`, perhaps we should all say what we were thankful for. I said I was thankful my family was safe and that I had found such a kind new family. Aunt Elsa said she was thankful that she had bought a couple of pumpkin pies just in case. And I can tell you, pumpkin pie is much more delicious than it sounds and much more delicious than steak and kidney pudding with whipped cream!

Good night, good luck and Happy Thanksgiving!

Edward

P.S. I wanted to say I was thankful for you too. I don't know what I'd do without your letters. You make home feel so much closer. Do keep writing, won't you?

P.P.S. Chicken names: Eglantine, Mrs Featherstone and Shelly. Shame you didn't keep one of the roosters, you could have called him Cluck Kent.

Captain Cricket Bat

Hailstorm Harriet

Dynamic Dachshund

Wonder Hen

Dear Teddy,

Merry Christmas! I hope you aren't too homesick? Thanksgiving sounds wonderful. I am very thankful for you too, even if America has turned you all sappy. What I wouldn't give for an enormous turkey and buttery mashed potato! I'd probably even eat the steak and kidney pudding. We don't get much meat and I've not seen whipped cream in forever, who's to say I wouldn't gobble it up like Frank?

I hope you are having a good Christmas. I wasn't allowed to send a present so I drew you this picture of us next Christmas instead. Do you like my new character? I didn't have as much time to finish it as I would like, because your mother insisted we post this early so that it would get there in time. I hope it does!

Best wishes,
Harriet and Wonder Hen

Dayton, Ohio

Dear Harriet,

Happy New Year! Help is at hand! President Roosevelt has promised to help Britain and the Allies win the war! He said so in one of his 'fireside chats' that we were listening to on the wireless. The president sounds like a very nice man and I certainly liked what he had to say and I'm extra glad he won the election.

He said Hitler was like a tiger and that there was no reasoning with him. Soon the USA would have no choice but to fight and that they had to get ready because Hitler isn't going to stop at Europe. Hitler wants to control the world and America needs to be ready to stop him.

He said that America's future depended on Britain winning in Europe. He said he would make sure we had everything we need to fight Hitler, boats, planes, tanks, all kinds of things.

It felt wonderful. Uncle Tom patted me on the shoulder and gave me a look that said, "What did I tell you?" We've got to win this thing, Harriet. I want to be home by next Christmas and perhaps with Roosevelt's help, I will be!

I love my Christmas card. I'm glad you included Frank because I think he is **SUPER!**

I did get some presents. I got my very own baseball bat, ball and a catcher's mitt, which is like a kind of cross between a glove and a leather basket they use to help catch the ball. Seems a bit of a cheat to me. We have snow here at the moment so it will be a while until I can try them out. I was getting pretty good when I practised with John and Adam.

I do get homesick. I can tell you, because I know you won't worry. But I miss and worry about Mother, Father and Leonard so much sometimes that I can't think straight. I'll find myself staring out of the window wondering what they are doing and worrying that Leonard could have been shot down, or captured by

Germans or worse...

I miss home. I miss school. I miss cricket and I miss running down the road to knock for you so we can go play or work on our comic. I miss you nagging me. You really weren't as bad at cricket as I said you were. You were actually pretty good. I couldn't tell you that though. It's weird that some things are easier to tell people when you are a long way away and you miss them.

John was in training for Christmas and I think the Mayers missed him a lot, but they didn't go on about it. I think they thought it would make me feel bad about missing my family and the danger they were in. John might be in the navy, but at least he's not at war.

Did you have a nice Christmas?

Good night and good luck!
Edward

13th January 1941
Battersea

Dear Teddy,

I'm sorry you're homesick. Christmas away from home must be hard, even if you do get good presents and better food. Ours wasn't anything special compared to other years, no Agnes or Aunt Lucy, but I was grateful to be with Mother. Your mother came for dinner with us and Leonard was home, too. I showed him the drawings you sent me and he was **VERY IMPRESSED**. He looked tired. He said he'd been flying a lot but that it was nice to have a few days to come home.

Mother invited the Adlers too because they don't have any family here, but they are Jewish and don't celebrate Christmas, so they said thank you but they wouldn't come. Mother felt a bit **SILLY**, because she knew that already, but said she would invite them over another time. I wish you'd been here. We had a fun time, but it's not the same without the lights or the delicious food. Rationing feels **EVEN HARDER** at Christmas. We'd always have a goose and lots of sweets. Aunt Lucy would come down and tell us how lucky we were to have so many. Hah! I used to think there weren't enough! Do you remember when Father brought home that chocolate orange on Christmas Eve? You had better remember, I had to use all my willpower to save you a piece.

I bet you got lots of sweets at Christmas. Save a couple for me!

They don't make chocolate oranges now, or almost any kind of chocolate. The factories have been taken over to make tanks and aeroplanes.[24] Imagine if all the factories in the world that made bombs and bullets made **SWEETS INSTEAD**! I wonder if Churchill or Hitler ever considered that? Everyone would be much happier if we stopped all the silly fighting and rationing and everyone could have their fill of sweets. Or perhaps they could still drop bombs, but they would be filled with **SHERBET LEMONS** and **SUGAR MICE**! Instead of running to the shelter when the sirens went, everyone would run into the street to see what kind of delicious treats were on their way. That sounds

24 Harriet thinks things are bad now, but in July 1942 sweets and chocolate rationing came into force and was limited to 55 grams per person per week, followed by biscuits in August of the same year. This ration wouldn't be lifted until 1953.

like **MY KIND OF WAR!**

The shops are short of everything but they are still having the January sales. I can't think what they will be selling. Mother is hoping she will be able to get her and Agnes some stockings which she said she can't find "for love nor money". Agnes said friends of hers saved their real stockings for very special occasions. The rest of the time they fake it by rubbing gravy browning over their legs and drawing a line down the back with an eye pencil![25] Seems a lot of fuss to go to if your legs are going to be cold anyway.

Do write soon and tell me your news. I need something to help

25 Silk that was used to make stockings before the war was needed to make parachutes for the troops and so women really did use gravy browning to make their legs look like they were wearing stockings.

me get through the Blackouts.

I don't know how long we can keep going like this. During the day things aren't so bad. I get up, grab a slice of the yucky national loaf with a thin sliver of butter and jam, and go to school or knock for Irena to go play around some of the bombsites. Sometimes I help Mother with the WVS. Marigold, one of her old school friends, works the searchlight for the local ATS.[26] She shines a light up into the sky looking for German aircraft so that the men on the machine guns can see the planes well enough to shoot them down. Imagine being one of the only people in the country allowed to **SHINE A LIGHT** up into the sky! I told Mother I would love to go and help Marigold one day. Mother laughed and said that if **I DIDN'T HAVE THE NERVE** to go into the shelter there wasn't much hope for me on a searchlight.

But it's not the bombs that I am scared of. Well, I am a bit. What really scares me, is being so close to other people in the shelter. Fear is dangerous! I can handle my own, and Mother's. But you can't know how Mr McAllister is going to react when he is scared, or the Wiggins or Leonora Watts for that matter. They are lovely people, but they seem a little less lovely if they're about to crush you in their stampede to get out.

Yours,
Harriet

---

26 The women's branch of the British Army was called the Auxiliary Territorial Service or ATS.

Dear Teddy,

I've not heard from you in a while, your mother said a letter may have been lost at sea. I suppose we have been pretty lucky with our letters so far, they have to travel a long way! Perhaps it's swimming around somewhere in the Atlantic after being blasted out of its envelope by a U-boat. I was going to wait a bit longer but I had to tell you all about what happened! You **WILL NOT** believe it!

I went with Marigold to 'man' the searchlight at ███████████████. Seems silly to say 'man' when Marigold is a woman, but hey-ho. Perhaps they will change that one day. This war is turning lots of things that used to be manned into things that are quite often 'womanned'.[27] As long as things aren't **GER-MANNED** I don't think I mind, but I would love to have a job as important as Marigold's when I grow up.

It was SO **EXCITING**. She said she didn't think it would be a busy night. But **THEN** we got word that an **ENEMY** aircraft had been detected flying south! The night was so clear and quiet it was hard to believe anything was on the way. ████████████████████ ████████████████████████

Marigold told me she had received lots of training on

---

27 As lots of men were away fighting, women had to step in and take on the jobs the men had been doing previously.

recognizing the shape of aircraft from their outlines. She stood behind the heavy metal wheel that looked a bit like a steering wheel on a car and turned it to move the light through the sky.

██

██

██

████████████████████████ that's when I heard it, a **LOW HUM** at first that grew **LOUDER** and **LOUDER**. The location devices were right, there was something coming and I was in just the spot to see it.

The **SIRENS HOWLED** and instead of darkness, everywhere I looked there was light. Marigold shone the searchlight up into the night like a **SUN**. Oh, it was **THRILLING**, and **TERRIFYING**, and **THRILLING**, and **TERRIFYING**. There wasn't time to decide which. Marigold told me to **RUN** to the shelter, and I was about to, but then her wheel got **STUCK!** She couldn't budge it and without her light, the men with the guns wouldn't be able to see where to fire. My heart was pounding, but I knew I had to help. I grabbed hold of the wheel with Marigold and together we freed it! She didn't tell me to go to the shelter after that, so I stayed put. The men had their guns trained up at the sky, following her beam. I held my breath and then suddenly a shape broke the beam. There was no way I could have told you what it was, before the **ACK-ACK-ACK** of gunfire ripped into the night.

After the firing finished and the all-clear sounded, Marigold said she would take me home. She said she didn't know how she would explain to Mother.

"Careless talk costs lives," I told her. "It can be our secret!" She laughed and said that, right now, my mother was scarier than a sky filled with bombers. Mother was angry, but not with Marigold, with herself for letting me go!

"I don't know what I could have been thinking," she said. "It was far too dangerous a place to send a child. I should have sent you to the countryside with the other evacuees or to America with Teddy. You won't even go into the shelter. I don't know what I'm going to do with you!"

She didn't send me away with the other evacuees because she

had been separated from her mother a lot when she was little and hated it more than anything. But, she said, if I wasn't going to go down to the shelter, she would have no choice. I don't want to be sent away, I want to stay here. If I want to grow up and do my bit in the way Marigold, Mother and Aunt Lucy do, I have to do everything I can to stay alive. My part right now is to **BE BRAVE**, so I can continue the fight. I've decided I will go into the shelter from now on.

I can't even begin to tell you how much I miss you. I'm glad the Americans will pitch in. I do hope they come and help our troops too at some point. Roosevelt is right, Hitler is a tiger that won't be tamed and if he gobbles us up, there will be nothing to stop him from leaping across the Atlantic and taking America, too!

I don't know what would happen if we were invaded. We get leaflets telling us what to do. We will know there is an invasion if we hear the church bells ringing and we have been told to go about things as normal. If we are on our way to work or school we are supposed to complete our journey. More just carrying on. Irena still hasn't heard anything from her grandparents. If Hitler keeps **BOMBING** us the way he is, I wonder why he would even bother to invade as there will be nothing left!

I hope I get to work the searchlight again, but I doubt Mother will let me.

From,
Harriet

Dear Harriet,

I can't believe you got to work the searchlight! Half of your letter had been crossed out in blue by the censor again. **VERY ANNOYING**. It happens to Mother's letters sometimes. It's **CRAZY** to think there are people whose job it is to read our letters. Though I don't suppose they read all of them. It would take **FOREVER**. I bet it was exciting. To look the enemy in the eye, well at least to look it in the aircraft. You were so brave to help Marigold with the wheel like that. **A REAL HERO!** I am so jealous. I feel terrible not to be doing more to fight the enemy. My brother is tearing up the night in his **SPITFIRE,** Mother is running around London helping people who have lost everything and father is goodness knows where in Africa.

I spoke to Aunt Elsa about it. She said a friend

told her that people across the country were taking part in something called 'Bundles for Britain'.[28] She said lots of people were getting frustrated about wanting to do more, so they were gathering together to knit and collect winter clothing to ship over there. They're raising money to buy medical equipment to send, too. Uncle Tom suggested I call his doctor friends. It would be easy for his colleagues to say no to him, but to hear the voice of a Brit whose family could come face-to-face with a Nazi invasion at any moment, and still say no... Well, they would have **COLD HEARTS** indeed!

I said I didn't want to seem like I was begging. Uncle Tom laughed and said, "It's the American way. You need to be direct! That Churchill's got backbone and I know you have too."

And do you know what? He was right. I practised the script we worked on together and called round his friends. My accent worked a treat! I felt shy at first, but I've managed to get all kinds of donations – medical equipment, bandages, even money so we can buy things to send.

Some of the girls I was evacuated with are making

---

28 Bundles for Britain collected donations and arranged for them to shipped to the United Kingdom.

things to send and are **KNITTING UP A STORM.**
You will **NEVER GUESS** who their team leader is:
ELOISE from the ship! I'm sure you can imagine how
much she **LOVES** that. Aunt Elsa is trying to teach me
to knit. I'm not very good, but I am improving. I know
it isn't much, but I feel so much better now I have
something to do for the war!

Goodnight and good luck!

Edward

3rd April 1941
Battersea

Dear Teddy,

Wow! I can't believe you're learning to **KNIT**! I don't think I would be more amazed if someone told me Hitler was learning to **TAP DANCE**. Bundles for Britain sounds wonderful. It makes me feel so happy to know that people far away haven't forgotten us. I hope Britain can return the favour one day. Though I don't think anyone would want anything I could knit!

Has baseball season started? I read a book about it in the library, and from what I can gather, it's really just rounders with cheaty, catchy gloves. Has all your practice with Adam and John paid off? Should it be Captain Baseball Bat now?

Irena and her family come to our shelter when the siren goes now. Theirs was damaged when a nearby house was hit last month. I still don't like going underground, but it's better with Irena. We like to draw together. Take a look at this picture she drew of Agnes. Doesn't she look like a villain?

Important War Work

by Irena

When Professor Adler comes to the shelter we don't get to draw much because he has us doing MATHS. He used to teach maths at a university in Poland and seems to think you can never have enough of it. Mother is **THRILLED**. She says if I work hard, I could have an important war job like Aunt Lucy's when I grow up, but I don't think I want to be stuck inside all day. I'd prefer to have a job where I'm driving around fixing engines or 'manning' a searchlight, not sitting around doing **HARD SUMS**. I'm not sure Aunt Lucy's job is that important anyway. I know Agnes says it is but ███████████████████████████████████

██

██ she **SWEARS ME TO SECRECY** one more time I'm going to start keeping the chickens in her room. That would put her in a right **FLAP!**

The raids are different now too. Mother says the Germans are sending more and more fighter planes to protect their bombers. They are still dropping lots of bombs, but the RAF have brought down so many of them that the Germans can't afford to lose many more.

There go the sirens again. Will it be drawing or more hard sums?

Write soon!
Harriet

20th May 1941

Ohio

Dear Harriet,

Oh Harriet! You were frightened of the shelter before and now you're having to do maths down there! That is really scary! The censors **BLOCKED OUT** more of your letter. Could you imagine if Lucy and Agnes really were doing something **IMPORTANT**?

I'm doing better at baseball. It's actually more fun than I thought. Not as good as cricket, obviously, and I didn't make the team this year, but I'm improving. I got my first home run at the park on Friday. I think Adam was more excited about it than I was. He told the story at least three times at dinner. Uncle Tom said he'd like to hear me tell it, but I just went red and said that it must have been an easy pitch. At least I don't strike out every time, now.

Not long until summer vacation. The Mayers have a lake house and said we are going to go there for a few weeks.

Good night and good luck,

Edward (Captain Baseball Bat)

Dear Teddy,

You got a home run! My book said that was the best thing you can do —
like knocking a ball for six! You are clearly much better at baseball than
you ever were at cricket. Only kidding.

We're going to visit Agnes in ████████████████████
██
████████████████████████████████

Mother thinks it will be a **NICE HOLIDAY** for me. I don't know
what she can be thinking. It's not like it's **DANGEROUS** in London right
now. **THE BLITZ IS OVER**. It's so nice to spend all night in my **OWN
BED** and not have to go down to the shelter. That is as good a holiday as
a month at the seaside!

I know summer won't be the same without you! Wasn't it fun
last summer? Setting up comic-book HQ in the shelter. Goodness that
feels a long time ago now, doesn't it? So much has happened.

Yours,
Harriet

Dear Harriet,

I can't tell you how much I miss you **TEASING ME ABOUT CRICKET**. Only kidding. I heard on the wireless the Blitz is over. Wouldn't it be brilliant if that meant the war was over soon, too?

What a summer! We went up to the lake house on Lake Eerie. Frank sat in my lap the whole way. I can't believe he didn't like me when I first arrived, I'm his favourite now. The lake house is much more basic than their home in Dayton but we have a room with bunkbeds and there's a little stove and an outside toilet. Lake Eerie is so big that it looks like an ocean, in fact I would have been sure it was an ocean if it wasn't for the fact the water wasn't salty.

They have a boat that we take out fishing. I **CAUGHT A FISH!** A type called a walleye. Adam said it would be good to eat so we took it back for dinner. It was yummy, but it could have done with a few proper chips.

Oh, and s'mores! I have to tell you about s'mores. We will make them for sure when I get back. You take a marshmallow and put a long stick up its bottom then and toast it over the campfire. To eat it, you squash the marshmallow on top of a piece of chocolate between two crackers that are a bit like digestive biscuits. The trick is to get your marshmallow all gooey in the centre and a little crispy around the outside without it catching on fire or falling off your stick.

I've not quite mastered it, but my `creations` still tasted **DELICIOUS.**

In the evenings Aunt Elsa and I knitted mittens for Bundles for Britain. I can almost do one a night now, and they **ACTUALLY LOOK LIKE MITTENS!** We are going to be sending so much. I'm really proud. I just hope it all makes it across the Atlantic in time for winter. Mittens aren't much use to anyone in spring.

Yesterday, Uncle Tom took us to Cedar Point, an amusement park around the bay. My favourite ride was **THE CYCLONE**, the biggest **ROLLER COASTER** I have ever seen. I didn't think I would be brave enough to ride it, but then I remembered Leonard and Captain Cricket Bat. What kind of flying ace would I make, never mind superhero, if I was too scared to ride a roller coaster? It was such a **THRILL!** It felt almost like being a **REAL PILOT, HURTLING** to the ground before **ZOOMING** up at the very last second. We rode it **THREE TIMES.** When this war is over and we are grown up I am going

to take you to Cedar Point, I think you would **LOVE**
it.

Goodnight and good luck,

Edward

P.S. School starts back soon. I can't believe I will
have been here **A WHOLE YEAR**. Did you think I
would be gone **THAT LONG?** I didn't. You won't
forget me, will you?

Dear Teddy,

I can't believe you've been away for **A YEAR!** Of course, I'm not going to forget you, and not just because I want you to take me to ride the Cyclone one day (which I do), but because you are **MY BEST FRIEND**. If anyone is likely to forget anyone it's **YOU FORGETTING ME**, what with your **NEW FRIENDS, ROLLER COASTERS** and **ALL-YOU-CAN-EAT S'MORES**. It sounds like you had a lovely holiday. I miss going on rides. I loved the rides in Brighton before they closed the pier.[29] Cedar Point sounds even better! I'm not looking forward to going back to school. Though there are hardly any children in my class because so many are in the countryside, Mrs Markham goes easy on us.

We did go up and see Agnes but we didn't get to spend as much time with her as Mother had hoped. She really is **VERY, VERY**

'Hailstorm Harriet' who?

CANDY

29 Palace Pier in Brighton was shut down and a big section dismantled in 1940 to stop it being used in a Nazi invasion.

BUSY. She said she was sorry, but there is just so much to do on the farm. The harvest has begun and it is **HARD WORK**. I was so tired when I got home I fell asleep before we had even had supper! Agnes said they have to work so hard because most of Britain's food before the war came from abroad, so now we have to **GROW IT OURSELVES**. I was actually quite proud of her. She looked different too, suntanned and strong. I guess her war work is pretty important after all. **DON'T YOU EVER TELL HER I SAID THAT THOUGH**. Oh, I wish I hadn't written it now, but I'm not starting this letter again. Perhaps the censors will take it out. Fingers crossed!

We hardly saw Aunt Lucy. She gets up early and comes back VERY late, sometimes after we have gone to bed. One night she didn't come back at all. She said she had lost track of the time. She didn't tell me anything about what she was doing, but asked questions about how I was doing at maths and gave me lots of puzzles to complete. She said it was important to keep my brain busy.

From,
Harriet

Dear Harriet,

Uncle Tom said America will be in the war before we know it. The president has ordered that any German ships found in US waters be sunk on sight.[30] I can tell Aunt Elsa doesn't like it when he talks like that. She is glad America is helping Britain, but she **DOESN'T WANT TO GO TO WAR.** I can't blame her, even though I know the Allies need America's help. She is worried about John. I know she is proud of him for joining the navy, but she doesn't want him to fight or put himself in any real danger. She's acting just like Mother when Leonard joined the RAF – completely **BONKERS.**

He is in Hawaii at the moment which is about as far away from the Germans as you can get. Adam said the Germans aren't a big threat over there, but the Japanese are, who are on the same side. Adam showed

---

30 Roosevelt made this order after a German U-boat attacked a US ship off the coast of Greenland.

me where Hawaii is in his atlas. It seems crazy to think that it is part of the USA. It's miles away!

I spend so much time thinking about Leonard and you and Mother facing the Nazis that I forget that this is a WORLD war and not just a British one!

Good night and good luck!
Edward

Dear Teddy,

I can understand why Aunt Elsa doesn't want a war. I know I don't! How was Halloween? We went to the church hall for a party. There was apple bobbing and some other games and a big plate of gingersnap biscuits, which were delicious and tasted like they were made with the proper amount of sugar! A real treat!

It will be Bonfire Night on Wednesday. Not that it's the same with the war on. No bonfire and no proper fireworks! People aren't too keen on fires and big explosions at the moment, for obvious reasons. I don't know what Mr Tavistock would do if you lit up a load of fireworks after Blackout! Hah it would almost be worth doing it to see him try and put a curtain over a Catherine wheel!

Mother has invited the Adlers over for indoor fireworks. They are nothing like the real thing. They are made of paper and float up to the ceiling when you light them, some of them wriggle around on a plate like worms leaving a small pile of ash, but there are no loud bangs, which is one hundred per cent fine with me.

From,

Harriet

12th December 1941

Ohio

Dear Harriet,

I'm sorry I haven't written for a while, so much has been going on. The Japanese bombed Hawaii! The US navy base at Pearl Harbor. Now, America is at war.[31]

Pearl Harbor is the last place John wrote from. Aunt Elsa sat wringing her hands as she listened to the news on the wireless. I felt a bit like an **INTRUDER**. I know how worried they must be about John. I am too. After the broadcast, I made an excuse and went up to my room so they could be together without me. Later, Uncle Tom came up and said that I should come back down. He said that although I had my own family I had become part of their family and **FAMILIES STICK TOGETHER** during times like these. We'd face **THE ENEMY** together. I just hope we hear John is all right soon.

31 The attack at Pearl Harbor was a surprise strike by the Japanese on America's naval base in Hawaii. The Japanese air force bombed the US ships, sinking four of them.

Roosevelt **DECLARED WAR** on Japan, and Germany have declared war on the USA. It feels like everyone is fighting everyone now. Surely it has to end soon?

Adam asked me what it was like to be at war. I didn't know what to say at first but I said it was like having a bit of your brain that was **ANGRY** and **SCARED** all the time, but that was just part of your brain. The rest of your brain got on with other things, like baseball and school and comics and arguing with your mother and father. And while all those plain old ordinary things exist, there is still America and Britain. It is what our brothers, our fathers, all of us are fighting for.

He punched my arm and said I was starting to sound like Churchill.

It will be funny when I go to school after the holiday. I hope people don't look to me as some kind of **"WAR EXPERT"**. I know I'm not as shy any more, **BUT STILL!**

A few things I have learned since being in America: everything is faster, bigger and louder over here and one thing Americans love more than anything else is being American. They talk about it **ALL THE TIME**, about what America is and what it isn't. Hitler must be bonkers to declare war on them. They and the Japanese are in for the **FIGHT OF THEIR LIVES**.

I guess we are all in it together now.

Goodnight and good luck to us both,
Edward

P.S. We just got a **TELEGRAM** about John! When it arrived I thought the worst, Aunt Elsa **SCREAMED** when she read it. But it could have been SO much worse. He has a broken arm and will be coming home for a little bit. I guess I will be sharing a room with Adam again for a while. It will be good to have John home and safe! Adam and John are like real brothers to me now.

Dear Reader,

Edward and I didn't write to each other much after America joined the war. Edward threw himself into working on the war effort in Ohio and Mother and I went to live with Agnes and Aunt Lucy. Fuel rationing meant that we wouldn't have been able to see them very much otherwise.

I didn't **WANT** to go, but Mother told me we could take the chickens and that we could perhaps get a pig, too. So, I didn't **'SWINE'** too much about it.

I missed London, but it was nice not walking past **BOMBED-OUT HOUSES** all the time. Mother helped Agnes out on the farm (so it was still all-you-can-eat turnips) and I made lots of friends at the village school.

I still couldn't wait for Teddy to come home though...

From,
Harriet

EPILOGUE
1945

Dear Harriet,

THE WAR IS OVER AND I'M COMING HOME![32]

I can hardly believe it. I'm not sure you are going to recognize me. I've gotten so tall and fat. Well, maybe not fat, but broad at least! Have you changed? I guess you must be quite the young lady now. Not too ladylike I hope. I want to teach you baseball!

I sail on Saturday and I'm not sure how long the journey will take, but I could very well be home before this letter gets to you. I can't wait to see you and Mother. Mother says I might find things quite different from how I remember and that, although the war is over, there is a long struggle ahead with rationing and rebuilding all the bombed-out buildings. I'm a bit scared of what I'm going to find. I've lived a different life over here. I'm so sorry I didn't write to you as much, everything just got so busy! I suppose it did for you too.

---

32 World War Two ended on 2nd September, 1945. In April of that year, Hitler had died and by May, Germany had surrendered. On 8th May, Britain celebrated VE Day – Victory in Europe. But it wasn't until the Americans dropped two atomic bombs on Japanese cities that the last of the Axis powers surrendered and the war officially ended.

I can't wait to get back, do you think we can start working on the *The Keep Calm and Carry On!* Again? I've so many ideas.

I can't believe I will really be coming home! After all this time.

Goodnight and see you soon!

Edward

P.S. Nobody has mentioned me sounding English in years, I bet I will sound like a total Yank to you. Please – BE KIND!

19th September 1945

Battersea

Dear Teddy,

I just heard from your mother that you are **COMING HOME!** I cannot wait to see you. I'm quite the chicken farmer now, so at least you'll have enough eggs! And we've got a pig too! Don't worry about not writing. It's not like I did either. War does make people very busy. Mother and I moved up to live with Agnes for a while so we could all be together. She's actually **QUITE NICE** now. We'll have lots of time when you get back to work on *The Keep Calm and Carry On!* I can't wait to hear all of your ideas!

Be sure to fill your boots with candy before you board though. Sweet rationing is still in full force. Bring lots for yourself and extra for me. I want first dibs on the Tootsie Rolls! You've made them sound so delicious that I think it would be **FRIGHTFULLY MEAN** of you not to.

Your mother didn't say when you'd be back exactly. More silly war secrets, not wanting to let people know when ships are coming and going. You would think we were done with all that now! Well, I suppose if it means you **GET HOME SAFELY**, I can put up with it one more time.

This letter will be waiting on your doormat when you get back.

And I'll be banging on your door **VERY** soon too.

I'm sure you will miss the Mayers very much. You've told me so much about them over the years, I feel like I will miss them too. I hope I get to meet them one day! As long as you are absolutely sure they are not spies. Haha!

Yours impatiently,
Harriet

P.S. Make sure you bring my *Beano* back! Haha! I bet that's long gone. I'll make do with one of those Action Comics you wrote about. At least we have some brilliant new ideas for ***The Keep Calm and Carry On!***

TRUE OR FALSE?

False

Harriet, Edward, Irena and their families are fictional, though families a lot like theirs certainly did exist. Their stories are based on real evacuees' letters and accounts of what the war was like for them.

Edward and Harriet's letters would have taken much longer to pass back and forth across the Atlantic. Some would have almost certainly got lost! That's if they survived the snooping censors at all, of course.

True

In September 1939, over two million children were evacuated from their homes in major cities and coastal areas to foster families in the countryside. In 1940, with many people in Britain believing that a German invasion could happen at any time, some families began to look further afield. Families in countries around the world sympathized with the British people and wanted to do something to help so they wrote to the British government, offering to open their homes and take in their children. These young people, like Edward in the story, boarded ships bound for the USA, Canada, South Africa, Australia and New Zealand. When the SS *City of Benares* was torpedoed by a U-boat on 17th September 1940, all of these schemes were abandoned. The oceans were too dangerous. The children would have to stay put with their new families for the 'duration' and many would not see their parents or friends again until the war was over.

Some families, like Harriet's, stayed in big cities believing that being separated from one another would be worse than facing the German bombings. What do you think you would have wanted to do?

Harriet's friend, Irena and her family, found safety in London. Staying in Poland would have been very dangerous for Jewish people like the Adlers. Hitler and the Nazis blamed Jewish family for many of the problems in Germany and made life very difficult for them. After the war began, the Nazis in Germany and the countries they had invaded, such as Poland and the Netherlands, forced Jewish people from their homes, taking them to places called concentration camps where they were killed. Irena got out just in time, but many Jewish people, like Irena's grandparents, did not. It is estimated that over six million Jewish men, women and children were killed during the war. The Nazis targeted other groups, too, such as Slavic people, Roma people and people with disabilities.

TOP-SECRET WAR WORK

Aunt Lucy wasn't real, but women like her did have VERY IMPORTANT jobs during the war. A woman who was a whiz at maths and solving puzzles like Aunt Lucy would have been a good fit at Bletchley Park, Buckinghamshire. Bletchley Park was the home of Britain's top team of codebreakers, where brilliant mathematicians worked day and night to decipher Germany's uncrackable Enigma code, used to send secret messages.

The hard work of the men and women at Bletchley Park meant the Allies were able to intercept and understand Germany's top-secret plans. Aunt Lucy would have been forbidden from talking about her work during the war until the 1970s when the information was declassified.

KEEP CALM AND CARRY ON

Harriet and Teddy's comic-book title, *The Keep Calm and Carry On!* is inspired by a now famous 1939 Ministry of Information poster. The poster was intended to motivate the British people in case of attack.

But, even though nearly two and a half million posters were printed, they were never widely released. The poster design was rediscovered in 2000 and has since been reproduced and made into other products such as mugs and tea towels.

EVACUEE OR REFUGEE?

Edward was a refugee. We use the word 'evacuee' in this book because that was the word used during World War Two. But Edward's story reflects that of lots of people who we call 'refugees' today. A refugee is a person who is forced by war or threat of violence to make a long, dangerous journey to a place of safety.

When people discuss refugees or 'people seeking asylum', it is important to remember that not so long ago, Great Britain was a country brought to its knees by war. Faced with the prospect of invasion, many British families chose to send their children across the world in the hope of keeping them safe from harm. Families like the Mayers in the USA, Australia, New Zealand, South Africa and Canada threw open their doors to British children in order to protect them.

But these doors were not open to everyone. In June 1939, a boat filled with more than 900 people arrived in Miami, USA. The people on board were Jewish and hoped to escape the Nazis. They were denied entry and their ship was turned around and sent back to Europe. Many of the passengers then settled in Great Britain, but a quarter of those on board later died in the Holocaust.

TIMELINE OF WORLD WAR TWO

1st September 1939:

Hitler invades Poland. The British government orders the evacuation of over two million children from coastal towns and major cities to the countryside.

3rd September 1939:

Britain and France declare war on Germany. Prime Minister Neville Chamberlain tells British people that they are now at war.

September 1939 – May 1940:

The Phoney War – little military action in Britain. Many children return home from evacuation.

8th January 1940:

Rationing in Britain begins.

10th May – June:

Blitzkrieg, Germany bombs Netherlands, Belgium and France and quickly invades much of Western Europe.

13th May 1940:

Prime Minister Neville Chamberlain resigns.

26th May 1940:

Dunkirk evacuations – Prime Minister Winston Churchill orders all sea-worthy vessels to sail to France to rescue stranded British troops from German-occupied France.

10th July 1940:

Battle of Britain begins. Luftwaffe (German Air Force) bombs British ports to weaken British Navy.

August 1940:

Battle of Britain continues – Luftwaffe begin to target British airfields to weaken RAF.

7th September 1940:

Luftwaffe begin bombing civilians. They target London and other major cities around the country day and night.

31st October 1940:

Battle of Britain won by the RAF.

5th November 1940:

Franklin Delano Roosevelt re-elected as President of the United States.

7th December 1941:

Japanese bomb Pearl Harbour in Hawaii, USA.

8th December 1941:

USA and Britain declare war on Japan.

6th June 1944:
D-Day. Thousands of Allied troops storm beaches in Normandy, France, to begin the liberation of France.

25th August 1944:
Germans driven out of Paris by Allied troops.

30th April 1945:
Hitler dies in his bunker.

4th May 1945:
Germany surrenders.

8th May 1945:
VE Day – Victory in Europe day. The war in Europe is declared officially over.

6th August 1945:
USA drop atomic bomb on Hiroshima, Japan.

9th August 1945:
USA drop atomic bomb on Nagasaki, Japan.

14th August 1945:
Japan surrenders.

2nd September 1945
USA accepts Japanese surrender. End of World War Two.

PEOPLE FROM HISTORY

Adolf Hitler
1889-1945

Adolf Hitler was a member of the Nazi Party and rose to power as leader of Germany in 1933. In 1939, Hitler ordered the German Army to invade Poland, starting World War Two. Hitler believed German people were superior to all other races and thought that certain other groups of people should be exterminated, including Jewish people, people with disabilities and gay people. He ordered them to be sent to concentration camps to be killed. Hitler and the Nazis lost the war and Hitler is said to have died by suicide in his bunker in 1945.

Winston Churchill
1874-1965

A former soldier and skilled writer, Churchill was first elected to Parliament in 1900. He was appointed First Lord of the Admiralty when Britain declared war on Germany in 1939. When Prime Minister Neville Chamberlain resigned in 1940, Churchill took the position. As Prime Minister, Churchill formed alliances with the United States and the Soviet Union (now Russia) to defeat the Axis Powers – Germany, Italy and Japan. Many consider Churchill to be the one of the greatest leaders of the twentieth century due to his strong leadership during World War Two.

Franklin Delano Roosevelt
1882-1945

When Roosevelt was elected President in 1933, America was in the midst of the Great Depression with many people unable to find employment. He put the country to work, creating big employment projects paid for by the government. When Great Britain declared war on Germany in 1939, the Depression and the memory of World War One meant many Americans did not want to fight. Roosevelt did everything he could to prepare the USA for a war he was sure was coming, whether America liked it or not. When the Japanese bombed the United States naval base in Hawaii, Pearl Harbor, in December 1941 Roosevelt declared war on Japan. Roosevelt died during his fourth term, just a few months before the end of the war. He was the longest serving president in American history.

The Wright Brothers
Orville Wright 1871-1948
Wilbur Wright 1867-1912

Orville Wright and his older brother, Wilbur, grew up in Dayton, Ohio. From a young age, they were fascinated by aviation and were skilled engineers. In 1903, the brothers successfully conducted the first controlled flight of a power-driven aeroplane, lifting their small-engine aircraft, made from wood and fabric, off the ground for twelve seconds. They went on to build and fly more complex aircraft and are considered the 'fathers of modern aviation'.

Edward R Murrow
1908–1965

Edward R Murrow became a reporter for the US broadcast company CBS in 1935 and was sent to head the network's European office in 1937. When war broke out in 1939, Murrow was stationed in London where he reported on the Battle of Britain, even flying with the RAF during a raid. Murrow brought many of the horrors of World War Two into the homes of Americans more than 3,000 miles away. People had never heard anything like it before. Murrow would end his broadcasts by saying, "Goodnight and good luck."

FURTHER READING

More stories about evacuees

Goodnight Mr Tom by Michelle Magorian

Back Home by Michelle Magorian

Carrie's War by Nina Bawden

The War that Saved My Life by Kimberly Brubaker Bradley

Why not also read:
My Best Friend the Suffragette

M. Forrest
26 Landow Road
Notting Hill
London

3rd January 1913

Dear Christine,

I hope I scribbled down your address correctly! My governess,[1] Miss Inchpole, thinks it's a wonder I can read my own writing, as she can make neither head nor tail of it. I'm starting to see what she means. Haha! It was **BEYOND WONDERFUL** to meet you outside the WSPU headquarters yesterday. I have always longed for a **REAL, LIVE** actual pen friend. I pretended my diary was a pen friend for a while, but it never wrote back. How <u>RUDE!</u> I hope you write back! Keeping a diary is totally different from being able to write to someone who knows exactly what it is like to be eleven years old. It's **SUCH** a frustrating age, don't you think? Old enough to understand what is going on, but too young to do anything about it. That's how I feel anyway.

Did you get in a lot of trouble with your sister? Jane, was it? She looked quite angry when she found me and my

---

1 A governess was employed by a family to live in the home and teach the children.

sister thawing you out beside the fire. Did you make it home for dinner?

I really don't think she had any right to be so cross. Leaving you outside in the **MIDDLE OF WINTER** while she chit-chatted with her suffragette friends, you could very well have frozen to death.

I don't think that would look very good for the Women's Social and Political Union.[2] Imagine the headline:

I had such a jolly time talking with you! Do you often go to WSPU events? My sister, Sarah, is becoming quite the radical.[3]

---

2 In 1913 women were not allowed to vote. The Women's Social and Political Union (WSPU) – nicknamed 'the suffragettes' – was an organization led by Emmeline Pankhurst campaigning for women to be granted the same rights to vote as men.
3 A radical is a person who wants to change the way things are done in society.

She's always dragging me along so she can learn more about the WSPU. Mother can't bear it. Usually Sarah takes me to the Kensington branch.

"I'm just taking Mary for a walk around Kensington Gardens," she'll call to Mother and Father as she pulls me out the door, but we always end up at the WSPU headquarters or at the WSPU shop where she meets with her friends and picks up a copy of *The Suffragette*.[4] There are **HARDLY EVER** any girls my age around for me to talk to, so I end up sitting like a Freda-no-friends and doodling in my sketchbook. I was thrilled to hear that you like to draw too! Please send me one of your pictures! I love drawing all sorts of things. This is our cat, Milly. We named her after Millicent Fawcett:[5]

Millicent Fawcett

4 The Women's Social and Political Union's official magazine. Each issue contained news, letters from the WSPU leader, Emmeline Pankhurst, to her supporters and information about upcoming events.
5 The leader of the National Union of Women's Suffrage Societies (NUWSS), Millicent Fawcett believed women could achieve the vote using non-violent campaigning.

And I love drawing things from my imagination, like me as 'Detective Inspector M. Forrest':

Father thinks I could be a cartoonist when I grow up, but I want to be a **GREAT DETECTIVE** like Sherlock Holmes and solve **GRUESOME MURDERS**.

Have you ever tried drawing funny pictures? I **LOVE** drawing them. They make me feel much better when I'm grumpy!

Like this picture of my brother, Edward. He and I went for a walk in Hyde Park this morning. He wouldn't stop chasing the poor pigeons off the path.

They didn't **REALLLLLY** attack him like in my picture, but I wish they had. That would teach him!

I asked Mother if I could write to you and she thought it would be a wonderful way to practise my handwriting. She said young women need to stick together. **HAHA!** I've put my address at the top of the letter. I hope you write back soon! It would be lovely to meet up properly one day, too.

Yours,

Mary Forrest

P.S. Are you a suffragette?